Unsteady Love.

Sairah Kat.

Unsteady Love

Dedicated to my almost lover,
The one who inspired these words.

Sairah Kat.

To all those who are going through a break up,

I hope you find comfort in these words.

Unsteady Love

Welcome to my collection of prose and poems;
My thoughts
And my feelings.

Influenced by my adventures,
Inspired by my experiences,
And prompted by my memories,

All with one of my dearest friends,
arguably, my almost lover.

He knows who he is.

This is **my** side of our story,
Our almost
Love story.

Sairah Kat.

My heart is in your hands now…

Table of contents

Chapter 1

What are we?

Unsteady Love

Tachycardia
Hyperhidrosis
Tachypnoea
Horripilation
Palpitations

-   *The clinical signs of infatuation*

Sairah Kat.

Your lips
So delicately coated
In a thin layer of vaseline
Pressed against mine
Our tongues intertwined

Oh please
Make this moment
We share
Last forever.

Unsteady Love

That Friday night
You came over
After I had a long week
I was exhausted

You brought me flowers
And made my bed

You folded my laundry
And massaged my back

You sung me a lullaby
And cuddled me tight
Till I fell asleep in your arms.

You took care of me
And made me feel special.

- *Isn't that what love is?*

Sairah Kat.

"We're just friends"

You whisper
Ever so lightly

As you lean in
And press your lips
Ever so gently
Against mine.

Friends.

That's all we are.

Just *friends*.

Unsteady Love

My hand is for you to hold
My lips are for you to kiss
My scent is for you to smell
My touch is for you to feel
My warmth is for you to embrace.
My heart is yours to love.

Please take care of it.

Sairah Kat.

I used to be scared of men
With big, muscular bodies.

I thought they only went to the gym
To grow their arms
So they could punch
And beat up women.

You were the first man
To convince me otherwise.

I always felt safe with you.
Always.

Unsteady Love

Wrap your arm around my waist.
Be possessive of me.
Make them jealous.
I am yours.
I am all yours.

-    *In my dreams.*

Sairah Kat.

I know we're sort of long distance
But just a little bit of extra effort
Will be so worth it.

-   *I promise*

Unsteady Love

"I miss you more than you know"
"Maybe we should give us a try"
"I like you more than I want you to know"
"I feel something more when I'm with you"
"You're so special to me"
"I want to spend forever with you"

   -   *Unsent messages*

Sairah Kat.

I wish you knew
That I wanted you.
I wish you knew
That I'd be willing to give us a chance.
But some things are best
Just left unsaid.

-    *Words I'll never say to him*

Unsteady Love

If you can't serve me your heart
Don't make a table
For me to eat at.
Don't give me a taste test
Of everything you have to offer.
I don't want to see
What I can't have.

Just leave me be.

Sairah Kat.

I don't know the difference
Between limerence and love.

But I do know for sure
Is that you don't love me
And you never will
At least
Never more than just a friend.
And that hurts.

- *situationship*

Unsteady Love

I know we're just friends

But it's the way

The way our hugs
Last a little longer
Than they should

The way our hands
Interlock
As we stroll through the mall

The way his arms
Hold my waist
As we're standing in line

The way our eyes meet
And stare
A little longer than they should.

-    *More than friends, less than lovers*

Sairah Kat.

I don't have to say the words
"I love you"
For you to know.

Back massages
Plucking your eyebrows
Messaging you "drive safe"

It's the little things
That I do for you
That scream
Those 3 words
Far louder
Than if I said them.

Unsteady Love

I want my last first kiss
To be with you
And only
You.

-    *Is that too much to ask?*

Sairah Kat.

I remember
The first time
You saw me
Without makeup on

You were silent.
And you remained silent.

While you stared
And stared
And stared.

While I waited
And waited
And waited

For at least a subtle compliment
To leave your lips

Instead
You looked away
And told me we should call it a night.

Unsteady Love

For a split second
It was just us
Our skinny love

Just me and you
In all our moments
of intimacy
and secrecy.

-   *Behind closed doors*

Sairah Kat.

We're just friends
We told each other
Over and over
And over
and over

But you and I
Both know

We stopped being "just friends"
A long time ago.

- *Our skinny love*

Unsteady Love

Maybe,
I don't want a relationship with you
But I really do
Like the experience I have with you.

Why do I feel this way?

Sairah Kat.

We're just friends
But we kiss so passionately
Our hearts intertwined
Beating in rhythmic synchrony.

Were just friends
But we held hands
Walking through our local shopping mall
Exposed and visible to those that know us.

We're just friends
But the line between friends and lovers
Was blurred.

Were just friends
Who were too afraid to be anything more
So we pretended we were not.

-   *Are we too afraid to love each other?*

Unsteady Love

I'd rather give it a shot with you
And have it end in tears and disaster.

Than to live my life
Wondering
What if?

- *Why can't we just try?*

Sairah Kat.

How many times will you message me?
How many times will you take me out for dinner?
How many times will you open doors for me?
How many times will you walk on the roadside?
How many times will you buy me flowers?
How many times will you drive me home?
How many times will you kiss me goodnight?
How many times will you tuck me into bed?
How many times will you hold my hand?
How many times will you play with my hair?
How many times will you massage my back?
How many times will you make love with me?
How many times will you cuddle me to sleep?
How many times?

Before we realize
we've gone too far.

- *This is too far*

Unsteady Love

Everyone warned me about not settling
For the man that gives the bare minimum.

Everyone warned me about not settling
For the man that speaks more than he acts

But no one warned me about the man
Who gives me his everything
Who treats me like his queen
But still doesn't want to commit.

-   *What do I do now?*

Sairah Kat.

You only ever told me I was pretty
When we were lying in your bed
Naked
Kissing
Touching

You'd let the words slip out
"You're very pretty"

But you never said that to me
When we were fully clothed
Doing something
Platonically

Unsteady Love

I traveled 321 km
To see you

To spend a day
With you

To eat dinner
With you

To share a bed
With you

To make memories
With you.

And I would do it all over again.

And you think
That I'm not in love with you?

- *Are you blind?*

Sairah Kat.

When you asked me to pluck your eyebrows for you
I really did think I was special

To be able to take care of a man,
My man (for the night),

You laid there
Patiently
On my bed

Not once did you ask to check in the mirror
You *trusted* me.

Trust.
Isn't that what love is?

Unsteady Love

Do you ever look at me
And wonder
"What if?"

Because I do
When I look at you.

Sairah Kat.

Please
Tell me you thought about me
Being your girlfriend
Your girlfriend.

Please
Tell me it crossed your mind.
At least once.
Just once.

Unsteady Love

Did you come back to me
Because
You loved me?

Or

Did you come back to me
Because
She didn't love you?

I should of asked you that question
Before
I let you back in…

-    *It's too late now*

Sairah Kat.

My heart is not a playground.
For fun and games
For you to stomp all over
For you to play with
Laugh with
And make great memories with.
Until you get bored.

So please
Don't treat it like one.

Am I asking for too much?

Unsteady Love

His thoughts
Her thoughts
She is so clingy and touchy
I love how affectionate he is
Why does she always complain?
I really like how he listens to me when I am upset
It's such an effort making restaurant reservations
I really appreciate the effort he puts into our dates
Ugh I have to make plans with her at least a week in advance
I really appreciate that he respects my busy schedule
She always needs reassurance over the small things
I really like how he communicates with me
She expects me to dress up to see her
I appreciate the effort he puts into his outfits
Nothing I do is ever good enough for her
He treats me better than any man ever has
I'm never going to meet her expectations.
Where else will I find a man that treats me this well?

-    *Incompatible love languages*

Sairah Kat.

I thought we were just friends
But every now and then I catch myself thinking about you
In ways that I shouldn't

I thought we were just friends
But our hugs last a little longer than they should
And I get this warm sensation through my body

I thought we were just friends
But I catch you staring at me for longer than you should
And I can't help but smile back at you

I thought we were just friends
But you lean across the dinner table just to kiss me
And butterflies tickle my tummy

I thought we were just friends
But you tuck a loose strand of hair behind my ear
And I feel my heart beating out of my chest

I thought we were just friends
But our hands interlock as we stroll down the busy high street
And I let my guard down

I thought we were just friends
But you kiss my forehead so delicately
And my heart begins to melt

I thought we were just friends
But friends don't act like that.

-    *So what are we?*

Unsteady Love

We were always on the verge of almost.
Never nothing,
Never something.
Between us was an almost "love story"

More than friends, less than lovers.

Sairah Kat.

Not all moments are meant to be understood.
Just like
Not all people are meant to be understood
So for now
Its best
We just enjoy what we have
Because we don't know
How much longer we have.

Unsteady Love

I don't really understand us.
What we are
What we have
Going on

But I do know
We don't know
How much longer we have.

We are running out of time.

Sairah Kat.

In the dark
Our bodies intertwined
Through all of our moments
Of intimacy

We lay next
To one another
Like we usually would

But we didn't know
That this time
Was going to be
Our last.

-   *all we have left is our memories.*

Chapter 2

What happened to us?

Sairah Kat.

You told me you needed some space
So I gave you space

But space
Turned into absence

And absence
Turned into you

Forgetting.

Who I was.

-     *What happened to us?*

Unsteady Love

We never had a label
"Were just friends"
We told each other

We never had a label
"Our undefined friendship"
We reassured each other

In the end,
I fell first,
He fell harder,
But for *another girl*.

-    *heartbroken*

Sairah Kat.

You had my heart
My love
My affection

My mind
My body
And my soul.

So why did you need her too?

Unsteady Love

I want you to know
You can always come back

I'll be waiting for you

Just in case
It doesn't work out

With *her.*

-     *I'll wait for you*

Sairah Kat.

I was going to tell you that I love you.
By making a playlist on your phone
Of our favorite songs
Titled
"Jeg elsker deg" *

To be subtle.

Subtle like our feelings for eachother.

But
You never let me touch your phone.

So I never got the chance to tell you
That I love you.

Translation:
* jeg elsker deg (Norwegian) = I love you (English)

Unsteady Love

Planned dinner dates days in advance
Restaurant reservations with deposits
Paying the bill
Picking me up and dropping me home
Meeting my parents
Opening doors for me
Walking on the road side of the sidewalk
Dressed in your finest clothes
Leaning over the dinner table to kiss me
Holding my hand
and
Late night cuddles.

If that's how good you're going to continue to treat me
After I tell you I like you,
And you still don't want anything serious with me,
Then f*ck you.

- *Why did you lead me on like that?*

Sairah Kat.

Why did you choose to break up with me
In my favorite bar
That I visit often.

I trusted you
When I took you there
That you would carry
The tradition of good experiences

And now
I can't even bring myself
To walk past it.

Unsteady Love

We got so close.
What happened?
What happened to us?

Sairah Kat.

I remember the first time you held my hand
And my first thought was

This is going to hurt
If I have to let it go.

-   *And I had to let it go.*

Unsteady Love

What was I to you?

A practice run?

An ego boost?

Sairah Kat.

Our pictures.

They could of fooled anyone
That we were in love.

Unsteady Love

That time you messaged me
That "we are lovers, in secret"

I would've believed you
If I didn't know
How much you like to joke around
With my feelings.

Sairah Kat.

I thought you wanted me.
Or maybe I just hoped
You wanted me
A little too hard.

Unsteady Love

You just liked the attention I gave you
More than you liked me.

Sairah Kat.

If finders are keepers,
And I found you,
Then why don't I get to keep you?

Unsteady Love

What did I do to make you decide I wasn't worth it?
When did you decide I was not enough?

Or was I always…

                              just never enough…

Sairah Kat.

You really meant something to me.
How naive of me
To think
That you felt the same.

Unsteady Love

When you joked we were lovers in secret
I had hope
Because that's how most love stories start.

And as our story went on
We became lovers.

Lover's without the L.

Sairah Kat.

You almost held my hand
I almost kissed your cheek
You almost told me your deepest secrets
I almost told you mine too
You almost called me your girl
I almost was only for you
You almost bought me flowers
I almost got princess treatment
You almost complimented me
I almost believed you
You almost treated me how I deserve
I almost let my guard down
You almost fell in love.
I almost waited.

We almost made it.

But almost
Was the farthest we could ever go.

-   *Did we give up too soon?*

Unsteady Love

I think
What hurts the most
Is that I thought
You felt the same

-   *but you never did.*

Sairah Kat.

This time he met my parents
This time he saw me naked
This time I told my friends
This time I opened my heart to him
But it was this time,
after all these things
He dumped me.

I guess I should have waited.
For the next time.

Unsteady Love

It makes me sick
Thinking about
How close we got
How well you treated me
How you made me fall for you

But I never really fell in love with you
I fell in love with who you pretended to be.

-    *Then you took off your facade*

Sairah Kat.

Its 8:45 pm on a Sunday night
And I'm sitting at my dining table
Wondering
What I could've done differently
To save
What we had.

And I'm not even on your mind.

Unsteady Love

It just doesnt make sense.

How can you treat a woman
So well
To put so much effort in
To planning our dates
And impressing me.

Consistently

To then decide
In an instant,
Out of nowhere
With no warning signs
Tell me
That you don't want me anymore.

- *What happened to us?*

Sairah Kat.

It was
Our undefined friendship
Our something in between
"Something in the middle"
Never nothing, never something
More than friends, less than lovers

I wanted something more,
But you said you weren't ready.

Unsteady Love

And just like that
You left.

Sairah Kat.

I know you only took me on 7 dates
But
You were the first man
That had treated me right
Treated me how I deserve
In four and a half years.

Please
Don't leave me now.

Please
I want to make this work with you.

Please
Don't tell me you're not ready for a relationship.

It's not fair.

Why did you lead me on like that?

Unsteady Love

When I set the bar high
For what i would accept
From men
That would take me out for a date

I never thought one
Would treat me so well
So perfectly
Only to turn around and say

"I did it for you because I thought that's what you
wanted."
"It's not how I feel about you"

And after that
I kept my distance
To avoid the men
Who are people pleasers.

- *Emotional manipulation*

Sairah Kat.

After taking me out
On the nicest dates
Over three months
You told me you weren't ready for a relationship.

But 2 weeks later
You updated your Facebook status
"In a relationship"
It was with *that* girl.

The one you told me was "just a friend"
The one you reassured me "don't worry about her"
The one you comforted me "she's not my type"

But

What happened to us?
Was I asking for too much?
Why wasn't I enough for you to be honest with me?

Unsteady Love

I was always told
That the way someone treats you
Is how they feel about you.

But him?
He treated me like his queen
He was the textbook definition of a gentleman.
He treated me exactly how I deserved.

And then one night
While we were on about our 10th perfect date
In a row
In 3 months

The truth slips from his lips
"I don't want a relationship with you"

So now what?
Now tell me what I do.
Tell me how to get into a relationship.

Because I have lost all trust.
All trust in any man.
That ever takes me on a date.
Ever again.

Sairah Kat.

That night I cried my eyes out
On your shoulder
Whilst lying in my own bed
With you by my side

I wanted nothing more than to hug you tight
To be held by you
And you couldn't even do that.

I don't think I've ever felt lonelier
Than in that moment.

But I hope you never have to experience that feeling.

Unsteady Love

It breaks my heart
That you weren't happy with me
Because I tried.

I really tried.

I tried so hard to make it work
To make *us* work.

But in the end
You knew what you wanted
And it wasnt me.

It was *her.*

Sairah Kat.

The way you held me
In your arms
The last night we spent together

I never would of imagined
That you were gonna leave me.

-    *Then you took off your facade.*

Unsteady Love

You tell me you're not ready for a relationship

But then
You take me out for dinner
You open doors for me
You cuddle me to sleep
You massage my back
You bring me flowers
You take care of me

Why did you do all these nice things for me?

Why did you show me what it's like to be your
girlfriend?

If all along,
you were too afraid of *commitment*?

Sairah Kat.

"I don't know why you thought this was going to turn
into a relationship"

But
The way you treated me
Like a queen
Like *your* queen

Would of fooled anyone
That you were in love
With me.

- *emotional manipulation*

Unsteady Love

The love we had for each other
Was so real.

Where did it go?

Chapter 3

Can we just try?

Unsteady Love

We only fail when we stop trying.
And I'm not ready to give up on us.
And what we have.
So please
Tell me you feel the same.

Sairah Kat.

Please
Tell me I nearly had you?

-   *I really wanted to call you mine*

Unsteady Love

It wasn't meant to end this way.
We deserve another chance.
We owe it to ourselves.

Sairah Kat.

How am I supposed to move on?
Move on from the idea
That we were meant to be.

When we never even *tried…*

Unsteady Love

Please
Can we just try?
One more time.

    -   *I beg you*

Sairah Kat.

Your left lung and your right lung.
They come as a pair.
They can work alone.
But together, they work best.

Your left lung is smaller than your right lung.
The left lung took the compromise
To make room for your heart.
It knew it was worth the sacrifice.

We are a pair of lungs.
You are the right lung
And I am the left.

Unsteady Love

You left
Just as easily
As a child would leave a toy
They're bored of playing with.

On the ground
In the middle of the living room.
Exposed and unprotected
Vulnerable to being kicked,
Stepped on
And broken.
By anyone and everyone walking past.

At least pack me up
Put me away
On the shelf
Ready for the next man
To open me up.

Sairah Kat.

Why do we keep running back to each other?

If we can't stay away from each other,
Then maybe we aren't meant to be apart?

Unsteady Love

It's never too late
To begin
 Over love again.

I'll wait for you.

Sairah Kat.

I am grateful,
For what we had.
But when can we finish *our* fairytale?

It's not supposed to end like this…

Unsteady Love

Why was I so afraid of losing what we had?
When we never had anything to begin with?

Why was I so afraid of losing what we had?
When what we had didn't matter to you anyways.

Sairah Kat.

Please,
Let me walk away first
So I don't have to watch,
Watch you walk away,
From me.

Our last goodbye.

Unsteady Love

To make a long story short.
The love we had for each other
Just wasn't enough to make us lovers.

-    *almost lovers*

Chapter 4

Why was I not enough?

Unsteady Love

Did you not find what you were looking for in me?
Was it because my perfume is sweeter than hers?
Or my eyes are green but you prefer her blue?
Is my hair too blonde and you prefer her brunette?
Or do you prefer her messy bun to my blown out waves?
Is it because you're intimidated by my career?
Or was I just not funny enough?

- *Intrusive thoughts*

Sairah Kat.

What was it that I couldn't give you?
What was it that made you love her, but not me?
Were you too intimidated by my career?
Did you want a girlfriend that is housewife material?

-   *More intrusive thoughts*

Unsteady Love

Why did you do all those nice things for me?
If you never planned on staying.

Next time I'll think *twice* about men
who treat me nice.

Sairah Kat.

He really did love me with his actions
And yet he still chose to leave.

-   *Now I'm lost.*

Unsteady Love

My mum kept warning me
To not break your heart
To not lead you on

Little did she know
That you didn't want me.

It was you
That was breaking my heart
All along.

Sairah Kat.

I'm not mad that you didn't want me
I'm mad that you acted like you did

When all along
You knew
You had no interest in me.

Unsteady Love

Telling me
You weren't ready for a relationship
Isn't enough.

I deserve a better reason than that
To justify your actions
Of treating me like a girlfriend.

Sairah Kat.

I see men who treat their girlfriends
of more than two years
half as well as you treated me.

And yet all that effort you put into me.

Was a waste of fucking time.

Because in the end
After all that
You didn't even want me.

You just acted like you did.

Unsteady Love

Growing up
My father always told me
"Never let a man tell you
he doesnt want you
more than once"

I wish I had listened.

    -   *Why didn't I walk away?*

Sairah Kat.

You told me you wouldn't be mad
If we didn't make love again

Because I was just a temporary comfort to you

I was just there to fill the empty hole in your heart.

Until you got the girl you really wanted.
All along.

- *heartbroken*

Unsteady Love

All I really wanted was to hear your voice.
But a phone call was too much.
For you to give me.

Sairah Kat.

I know there will be another man out there
Who can give me
Everything I need
Everything I want

                                           and

Everything *I deserve*

And he won't make me feel like I am asking for too
much.

But right now
I really wish I was good enough for you.

Why am I not good enough for you?

Unsteady Love

You were such a good kisser
And you *knew* it.

I wasn't the first girl who told you that
And I know
With an *aching* heart
I won't be the last.

Sairah Kat.

Maybe in another lifetime,
You'll have my number saved as "wifey"

Unsteady Love

In another life,
You'll be the father to my children.
To *our* children.

-    *oh what a good father you would make*

Sairah Kat.

In another life
You'd d ask me to be your girlfriend

We'd fold the laundry
Cook, clean, vacuum together

In another life
You'll ask me to marry you

We'd get the kids up in the morning together
And laugh,

In another life
It would be me and you
Against the world.

In another life,
But not in this one.

Unsteady Love

In another life,
I'll be hearing my name
With your last name

But in another life,
It'll be for real.

Sairah Kat.

I cant wait till I find a man
Who treated me as well as you did
But this time,
He will want to stay.

Unsteady Love

You've told me twice now
That you don't want me

The first time
Was when you fell for her.

The second time
You weren't ready for a relationship.

Now I've learnt.

And I won't put myself in a position
For you to tell me
A third time.

- *moving on*

Chapter 5

How do I move on?

Unsteady Love

How am I supposed to move on from you?
How am I supposed to forget you?
How am I supposed to find a new lover?

When I don't even *want* to.

- *I want you, and only you.*

Sairah Kat.

You raised my standards so high
I'm afraid I'll never find a man
Who treats me half as well
As you did.

Why did you have to leave?

Don't try to convince me we weren't in love.
Friends don't act like that.

-   *emotional manipulation*

Sairah Kat.

Maybe you didn't come into my life for us to be together
Maybe you came into my life
To show me
How I deserve to be treated.

How a good man
Will take me out on dates
The way that you did.

But what kind of lesson is that?

Unsteady Love

Here I am
Sitting here
Writing this poem
And many others
And there you are
Not even thinking
About me.

Im sitting here hurting
And you're doing
Just fine.

-     *It's not fair*

Sairah Kat.

Maybe we weren't compatible all along.
Maybe I just loved the idea of you.

The idea of *us*.

But really
Maybe we were
Such a bloody good idea.

Why didn't we try?

Unsteady Love

I think
I fell in love
With the idea
Of what we could have been.

An idea
Made up in my head
In my imagination

And now I'm paying the price.

Sairah Kat.

Here's a page for you.
A page for you to write an apology.

The apology I *deserved.*

Unsteady Love

Sairah Kat.

The day you left
I drowned my heart
In peanut oil
To protect it
To prevent you
From coming near me
Even if you wanted to.

-   *He's severely allergic to peanuts.*

Unsteady Love

I am not a paper plate.
I am not a tampon.
I am not a tissue.
I am not a paper straw.
I am not a coffee cup.

You can't just dispose of me
After you've finished *using* me.

Sairah Kat.

I crave the day
When you stop being on my mind.

How much longer?
When is it coming?

Unsteady Love

I miss you
But I don't want you back.

Not after the way
You chose to leave me.

-   *It was your choice.*

Sairah Kat.

The way things ended between us,
Destroyed our good memories too.

Unsteady Love

I hope you regret
the way you ended it.

I hope you regret
the way you made it feel

Like all the love we shared
was a waste of time.

Sairah Kat.

I know I deserve better
You know I deserve better
Than to be fooled
By your facade.

Unsteady Love

Honestly
If your career in finance doesn't work out for you,
Consider acting.

Because your fucking great at it.

Sairah Kat.

I prefer to have conversations with you
in my head.

Because unlike in reality
You actually *listen* to me.

Unsteady Love

Give me back the love I gave you.
You didn't want it.
So it's not yours to keep.

Sairah Kat.

My heart still *aches* when I hear your name.

How unfortunate
That you have such a common name.

Unsteady Love

I think
We will always be
A little drawn to each other

As we live our lives in parallel
Glancing over at each other
From time to time

Our eyes interlock
Flashbacks of our memories
Flicker through my mind
Through your mind
Of what we had
And what we could have been.

Sairah Kat.

You will miss me
When you need a shoulder to cry on and I'm not there
anymore.

You will miss me
When you want to share your good news with someone
who truly cares.

You will miss me
On cold, lonely nights when the warmth of my body is
no longer yours to embrace.

You will miss me
When you're feeling down and need some soft, tummy
loving care.

You will miss me,
You just don't know it yet.

Unsteady Love

If you ever feel lonely
Just remember
I was willing to give us a try
I was willing to figure things out.

It was never me vs you.
It was always us vs the problem.

You just gave up too soon.

Sairah Kat.

I was always cautious
That look's can be deceptive.

Chocolate chips look like raisins
Sugar look like salt
Water looks like vodka.

So how ignorant I was
To think your lust was love.

Unsteady Love

I never fell in love with you.
I fell in love with the what ifs.
I fell in love with what we could have been.

I fell in love with your potential.

Sairah Kat.

Your scent still lingers on my bed sheets
From the last night we spent together.

And now I can't bring myself to wash them.

Unsteady Love

All along it was her.

Her.
That you really wanted.

And I
I was just there.

There
To fill the empty hole in your heart.

While you waited
Waited for her.

To come along

The one you wanted.
All along.

Too bad that empty hole in your heart
Only grew bigger.

When she left.

Left you.

- *Bandaids don't fix bullet holes.*

Sairah Kat.

I still have
The receipts from our meals
Our photos in my camera roll
And the memories in my heart.

It's not enough but at least it's something.

Unsteady Love

It was supposed to be us.
Please,
Tell me
It was supposed to be
Us.

Sairah Kat.

There's still nights that I spend
Holding onto our memories
Of what we had

And I look through the pictures
Of what we once were

And I wonder

Why didn't we try?

Unsteady Love

Am I crazy to think there is more to us?
Why do I keep wondering?
Maybe we aren't meant to be apart?

-     *Unfinished business*

Sairah Kat.

Pretending we never had anything

\-   *That's what we do best*

Unsteady Love

In another lifetime
You'll rock up at my doorstep
With the biggest bouquet of roses
I have ever seen
And a handwritten card
With a sheepish grin on your face
And like music to my ears, you'll say
"I'm sorry that I left you, but I really do want you to be
mine"

- *In another lifetime, but not in this one.*

Sairah Kat.

Why was your signature scent
Such a popular cologne

I find myself drawn to the men
Who wear it too.

-   *I spend my days looking for you.*

Unsteady Love

Whatever it was that took you away from me
I hope it makes you happy.
I hope it was worth it.

- *empty*

Sairah Kat.

I'm not interested in the man that wants last minute dates at
the local bistro
When you always made fancy restaurant reservations weeks
in advance
I'm not interested men that want me to meet him at the
restaurant
When you always drove 45 mins to pick me up to take me to
the restaurant.
I'm not interested in the man that makes me walk down the
road to the gelato shop
When you would book me an uber so I didn't have to walk
500 meters in heels.
I'm not interested in the man who wears jeans and a t-shirt on
dates
When you always dressed immaculately in a business shirt,
chinos and RM boots.
I'm not interested in the man that texts me "i'm here" when he
picks me up
When you would always come to my front door to pick me
up.
I'm not interested in the man who sends me flowers on
occasion
When you always made sure my vase was never empty.
I'm not interested in the man who talks to me when it's
convenient for him
When you always made time for me when I needed you.

You taught me a love I now yearn for.

Unsteady Love

I guess you were never mine to keep.

You were never mine to begin with.

Sairah Kat.

You wanted to just be friends
And you got exactly that

So stop trying to touch me
Stop trying to flirt with me
Stop trying to impress me

You got exactly what you wanted
"Just friends"

That doesn't extend to "friends with benefits".

- *keep your hands off me.*

Unsteady Love

Dont text me
You're insecure about your body.

Dont text me
You don't like your haircut.

Dont text me
You're insecure about the acne on your face.

Don't text me
You're not smart enough.

Don't text me
You're not fit enough.

You had a woman
right in front of you.
Who thought you were perfect.
Just the way you were.
Everything she wanted
Everything she needed.

That woman
Was me.
And you let me go.

So don't text me for validation.
It's not my job.

Sairah Kat.

And when he kisses me
On parts of my body
That were ever meant for you

What defenses do I have?

All I can do
Is to pretend
It's *you*.

Unsteady Love

I picked up
The pieces of my shattered heart
That you left on your doorstep
My hands
Too calloused
Too fragile
To get all the pieces home
I sit in front
Of my fireplace
And one by one
Begin stitching
The pieces
Back together.

    -   *healing*

Sairah Kat.

At first your slow replies
Made me crave your attention more
But then I just got bored of you.

Unsteady Love

What a shame everything you invested into me
Went to waste
You really had me as yours
At one point in time.

Sairah Kat.

I fell out of love,
When you stopped putting in effort.

Unsteady Love

My heart is no longer in your hands anymore.
What a good feeling.

Now I'm free.

Sairah Kat.

Today I woke up and you weren't the first thing on my mind.
I've been waiting for this day for a while.

- *10/08/2024*

Unsteady Love

I think
There will always be
That *ache* in my heart
Whenever I think of you

-    *I hope you feel it too.*

Sairah Kat.

I'll hold onto our memories
Forever,
And ever,
Because that's all we've got left.

-    *That's all you left me with.*

Unsteady Love

On my lonely nights
Our pictures take me back.

To what we had.
To what we once were.

And I grieve.
And I question.

Why didn't we try?

Sairah Kat.

Sometimes I wonder
What thoughts
Come to your mind
When you see the old pictures of us.
The photos we both have on our phones.
Somewhere in our galleries.

The pictures of us
Lying together
In my bed
Naked
Giggling

Our little moments
Of intimacy
That we captured

Just for us
Just for our eyes only
To look back on

Why did we take them?
Do you treasure them as much as I do?
What thoughts come to your mind?
Do you have to choke back that lump in your throat?
Or would you delete them just to free up storage space?

I don't think I could bear hearing your answer.
If it is going to be anything other than the words that
I want to hear.

Unsteady Love

That picture I drew of you,
Tell me you still have it in your draw.
Please,
Tell me you didnt get rid of it.

It meant a lot to me.

Sairah Kat.

I would do anything in this world
To press my lips against yours
Just one last time.

Please?

Unsteady Love

I guess hearts like mine
Are just meant to be
b-r-o-k-e-n.

Sairah Kat.

To you and your future girlfriend,
I hope she gives you what you need
I hope she gives you what you want
I hope you get that promotion you deserve
I hope you buy the house you've been saving for
I hope you have the children you've always wanted to
have
I hope you buy the car you've always dreamed of
I hope you stay healthy fit and well, both mentally and
physically
I hope those around you support you and your dreams
I hope you treat her as well as you treated me.
I hope she appreciates the dates you plan and the places
you take her
I hope you're out there smiling the way you used to.

Genuinely,
From the bottom of my heart
I wish you all the best.

My *almost* lover.

-    *Cheering for you from the sidelines.*

Unsteady Love

I would do anything in this world
To be held in yours arms
Just one last time.

-   *Please?*

Sairah Kat.

At least you gave me the bragging rights
Of telling people how well you treated me
And how high my standards are
Because of you.

-   *gratitude*

Unsteady Love

If we really are meant to be
We will meet again
But right now
I have to let you go
Until
You are ready
To come back
To me.

Sairah Kat.

I hope one day
I can feel some type of way
About you again.
And hopefully next time
It'll have a happier ending.

Unsteady Love

Maybe.
One day,
It'll end with us.

-     *I still have hope.*

Sairah Kat.

Maybe one day
We will meet again
With open hearts
And you'll feel some type of way about me
And I'll feel that same kinda way about you
And next time
I'll be able to write
Our story
With a happy ending.

My fingers are crossed.

Unsteady Love

"He'll come back"
My friends reassured me.

-    *but you never did.*

Sairah Kat.

You'll be the one left with our memories.
You'll be back
And I won't be there.

- *gone*

Unsteady Love

You treated me so well.
I lost all interest in any other man
On this entire planet.
You've ruined other men for me.
That's how well you treated me.

Sairah Kat.

You always protect me.
You always drive safely with me in the car.
You always respect my body.
You always ask for permission to touch me.
You never raise your voice at me.
You never get aggressive towards me.
You never try threatening me.
You never make me feel endangered.
You never raise your fists at me.
You never make me feel scared or powerless.

I always feel safe with you.

The way it should be.

I wish every women felt this way
in the presence of men.

I'm grateful that you showed me
There are good men
in this cruel world.

Thank you.

And all I have now.
Is to be grateful for how well you treated me.

- *You validated my high standards.*

Sairah Kat.

January 2024

My mum still asks about you sometimes.

You broke her heart too.

Unsteady Love

I think you may be
One of the best and worse things
That ever happened to me

How you dare leave my heart
Shattered into millions of pieces

But without you
These words would never of appeared on paper

Without you
These words would of stayed in the jail that my brain is
Never to be released.

Without you
There is no inspiration coming from me.

Sairah Kat.

I miss you
But I don't want you back.

I cry about you some nights
But I don't want you back.

I crave your hugs
But I don't want you back.

Unsteady Love

I'll always remember you;
My almost lover.
My skinny love.
The one that got away.

I hope you remember me too.

Sairah Kat.

I don't want to live my life
Waiting for you to decide
If you can live your's without me.

So I left.

- *Self respect.*

Unsteady Love

I'd rather be the girl you remember,
Than the girl you love half heartedly.

-    *I deserve better.*

Sairah Kat.

It doesn't matter how bad you treat me.
Or how mad you make me.
Your secrets will never leave my lips.

- *I promise.*

Unsteady Love

The more distance between us
The less contact you have with me.
The more I learn
That I am fine
Without you.

Sairah Kat.

You taught me that I am fine without you.
And I didnt even want to learn.

Unsteady Love

If a man really wanted you
He will make sure that,
No other man has access to you.
No other man can touch you.
No other man can impress you.

If a man really wanted you
He will do anything
To not lose you.

-    *A gentle reminder to myself*

Sairah Kat.

"Goodbye"
My (almost) love(r).

-    *you were never mine but I wish you were.*

Unsteady Love

I'm glad I met you
My dear friend.
And I'm grateful
For all the good times we spent together
My love.

But here's to finally moving on.

Sairah Kat.

I no longer have space
For you in my life
My love,
But you will always
Have a very special place
In my *heart*.

Unsteady Love

I don't want to know
How you are
How your day was
Or what you've been up to lately

But I will always hope
That things
Are working out
For you.

I wish you the best.

And I mean it.

- *Rooting for you from the sidelines*

Sairah Kat.

My heart no longer skipped a beat
When I heard your name
When you texted me
When I thought of you
And that was when
I realized
I had moved on

Now I'm free.

Unsteady Love

They say not all stories have a happy ending
It's true.
Our story didn't have a happy ending.
Nor did it have a happy beginning.
Or a happy middle.

But our story taught me a lot
About myself
And about you
And for that alone.
It is a story
Worth remembering.

I hope you remember us too.

Sairah Kat.

I like to think that
In the end
What we had
Was love.

Unsteady love.

But
At least
It was still
Love.

Unsteady Love

Love.
For what we knew it to be.

Sairah Kat.

Finishing this book
Submits to finishing
As if
To end
Our almost
Love story.

A thought
That I cannot begin to fathom

So

Just in case
One day
You come back

I'll leave a couple of pages
Blank
So we can continue writing
Our fairytale.

And next time
I'll be able to write
Our story
With a happy ending.

-    *I still have hope*

Unsteady Love

To be continued....

Sairah Kat.

Unsteady Love

Sairah Kat.

About the Author

Sairah Kat is a poet from Australia, writing prose/poetry from her break up experiences. Unsteady love is her debut book, inspired by her first heartbreak. She hopes to share her work with others who are going through a similar experience and to bring her audience together to support each other through this tough time of moving on and healing. Feel free to follow her journey on social media.

Join her community via social media:

Instagram:
@justagirlandherbrokenheart

Pinterest:
@justagirlandherbrokenheart

TikTok:
@sairahkatpoetry

Website:
www.justagirlandherbrokenheart.com

Afterword

Whilst dating the man who this entire book is about, my emotions were running high with confusion, lust, gratitude, uncertainty ect. So my way of processing my thoughts started by writing it out which gradually became more poetic in nature.

I continued writing when he broke up with me as it was my outlet for my feelings and allowed me to process my thoughts. As the months went by I wrote 300+ poems from us dating to the heartbreak I was experiencing from the breakup, I read through what I had written in the order that I wrote it and I noticed the poems took me through the different emotions I experienced after a break up. So I more or less kept the prose/poems in the order that they were written in throughout my book, as this best reflects my experience following the break up.

I wrote this book as my way of expressing my emotions following a difficult break up with a man who I wanted more with. As I continue to heal and grow following the break up, I aspire to continue writing poetry that reflects this change and explores these themes.

Sairah Kat.

Acknowledgement

To my almost love, the one this book is about.
You know who you are.

You are my greatest paradox.

The one who led me
To heartbreak,
To tears,
To pain.

But you also led me
To discover a new side of me;
A writer,
A poet,
An empathist.

Without you,
I would have no inspiration for these words,
And no success to follow it.

So thank you.

Thank you for breaking my heart.

I've become a better person because of it.

I'd also like to make a special mention to the very small handful of close friends who I told about this little project whilst wholeheartedly supporting me through the break up.

To some extent, I'd argue breaking up with someone who you have just started seeing for a couple months in some ways can be harder than someone you've been with for a while, as I was challenged by my thoughts of what if and the potential that our relationship had.

Being treated so well by a man and then ending on such good terms was challenging, even for my friends when it came to giving me advice.
I'd like to make a special mention to my dear friend, L.Z (her initials only) who honestly gave me the only piece of advice that made me feel better in the time I was grieving. She said;

"If thats how well a man will treat you, and he doesn't even want you, then imagine how well a man will treat you who does want you"

This.
To this day.
Has stuck very close to my heart.
And I remind myself of this all the time.

Sairah Kat.

www.ingramcontent.com/pod-product-compliance
Lightning Source LLC
Chambersburg PA
CBHW032032040426
42449CB00007B/866